Saint Anthony of Padua

of Padua

Proclaimer of the Good News

auline
BOOKS & MEDIA
BOSTON

Written by Marie Baudouin-Croix

Illustrated by Augusta Curelli

Translated from the original French by Sr. Maryellen Keefe, OSU

Edited and adapted by Patricia Edward Jablonski, FSP

*Layout:*La 7e HEURE

1998, Éditions du Signe, 1 rue Alfred Kastler, B.P. 94-F 67038 Strasbourg

Printed in Spain by Beta-Editorial S/A Barcelona

Other titles in this series:

Saint Thérèse of Lisieux
and the "little way" of love

Saint Colette
In the footsteps of Saint Francis and Saint Clare

Saint Francis of Assisi
God's gentle knight

Saint John Bosco
The friend of children and young people

Saint Vincent de Paul
Servant of Charity

This is the amazing story of Saint Anthony of Padua.

Before beginning to read it, turn to the back of the book. There you will find an explanation of some words that may be new to you.

Anthony's life was full of surprises. Sometimes he thought God wanted him to do one thing. Later he would find out that God wanted something else instead. But Anthony was always ready to cheerfully do whatever God wished—even when it wasn't easy.

Saint Anthony especially showed the love of Jesus by preaching his Good News to people who were poor, suffering or confused in any way. He wants to help you become more and more like Jesus and grow in love too!

The little boy who was to become Saint Anthony was born in Lisbon, the capital city of the beautiful country of Portugal. Portugal, located on the edge of the Atlantic Ocean, is a land of fishermen and sailors. Some have gone on long trips and have discovered faraway places on the other side of the ocean. Others have spread the Gospel around the world.

This baby boy was born over 800 years ago, in the summer of 1195, and baptized Fernando, which means "enthusiastic defender of peace."

Fernando grew up, almost like a little prince, in the close circle of his family, inside a big palace. His father, Don Marino, was a knight and a relative of Portugal's king.

Fernando's parents were very religious. They taught him as a very young boy how to pray and love Jesus. His mother, Maria, often told him the story of Jesus, the Son of God, who came to earth out of love for us. Fernando grew up happily under the loving eyes of God.

But his upbringing was strict. At an early age he was taught how to share with the poor, to have good table manners and to be polite at all times. A knight's son was expected to be brave and good and kind.

Fernando enjoyed horseback riding and was often seen galloping across the sunny fields. Maybe you would have liked to be one of his friends and ride with him over the wide plains and the sandy sea-shores!

One time Fernando rode across the fields with his father. They were going to visit one of the farmers. The cornfields were ready for harvesting, but suddenly a large flock of sparrows flew down and began eating all the corn. Fernando's father was worried. Something had to be done to save at least part of the crop.

While his father hurried to tell the farmer about the problem, Fernando tried to make the birds go away. But nothing worked. Finally, Fernando went to a nearby chapel to pray. He called the birds to follow him. Imagine how surprised his father was when he came back and found Fernando in the tiny chapel—surrounded by all the birds!

Soon Fernando went to study at a monastery. The monks were very well-educated men who belonged to the Order of St Augustine. Fernando's uncle, whom he especially admired, was a priest there. The sons of knights did not have to attend school in those days, but Fernando was very eager to study.

Day by day, Fernando's desire to become like the monks grew. He wanted to serve God in the monastery. He talked to his parents about his dream. They had hoped that he would become a knight of the king, like his father, but at last they agreed. Fernando would enter the service of God, the Creator and King of the world.

At the age of fifteen, Fernando entered the monastery of the Augustinian monks in Lisbon in order to give his life to God. As a new monk, he was called a "novice."

His friends often came to visit him. They told him about their adventures and all the latest news. They talked and they joked. This disturbed Fernando in his chosen life of quiet and prayer.

He so much wished for peaceful silence so that he could hear Jesus and talk with him, that he asked the abbot to send him to a different monastery, far away from Lisbon.

And so Fernando moved to Coimbra, where he contin-
ued his education. Through studying and praying, he
prepared to become a priest.

The monastery of Coimbra had a wonderful library, with thousands of valuable books. How exciting it was to go there and read, learn and think! Books were one of Fernando's greatest interests. His favorite book was the Bible. It is said that, later on, he learned it by heart!

At last, Fernando was ordained a priest. He would serve God faithfully in obedience and live in poverty and chastity. As a young knight he had been helped by servants. But from now on he would serve everyone. Fernando was filled with happiness!

His job was to welcome visitors to the monastery, whether they were famous people or poor beggars. He received, with a smile, everyone who knocked on the door. But the poorest people made him feel closest to Jesus. He gave them bread, soup and kindness.

However, in Coimbra, there were some brothers from rich families, who preferred an easy life. They accepted fancy presents and lived by their own rules, ignoring the rules of the monastery. This displeased Fernando very much but he did not criticize them. He remained faithful to his job and did his work carefully.

Around this time some men called "the Little Brothers" came to Coimbra. They followed the rule of Francis of Assisi. (After his death, Francis would be canonized a saint.) The Little Brothers chose to live in poverty, in imitation of Jesus, and to beg for what they needed.

One day, five of these brothers arrived at the monastery in Coimbra. Fernando welcomed them. They were passing through on their way to Africa. They intended to go to Morocco and preach the Gospel.

Later, while they were spreading the Christian faith in Morocco, these followers of Francis of Assisi were put to death. Their bodies were brought back to Coimbra and buried in the chapel of Fernando's monastery. Now the five brothers were honored as martyrs.

Fernando was impressed by the Little Brothers' way of life. All that had happened convinced him that he should follow the martyrs' example. Like them, he wanted to become a missionary and spread the love of Jesus. In the name of God he would risk all—even if it cost him his life.

It wasn't easy to get his community to let him change to a different order. After first saying "No" and "Maybe," the abbot finally said, "Yes."

One of the monks said as a joke, "I suppose you want to become a saint?" Fernando answered him very seriously, "If you hear one day that I have become a saint, thank the Lord!"

Fernando said good-bye to the other monks, took off the white habit, or special robe, of the Augustinian monks, and dressed in the rough brown woolen habit of the Little Brothers of Francis! As part of his new life he also changed his name. He was no longer called Fernando. His new name was Anthony.

Anthony wanted to go to Morocco as soon as possible, following the example of the five martyrs. His superiors knew how much this meant to him and they allowed him to set out on this mission.

Ahead of him was a long, tiring and dangerous journey.

Finally, Anthony arrived in Morocco. But he couldn't take the terribly hot climate and the extremely hard life of the missionaries. He fell ill soon after his arrival. Even with the best of care, his fever wouldn't go down. All through the winter and far into the spring he had to stay in bed.

What did God want him to do?

His superiors realized that Anthony could never get well in Morocco's climate, and so they called him back to Portugal. Once again, he boarded a ship. And once again God let Anthony know that there would be new surprises in his life.

A fierce storm broke out at sea. Anthony's ship drifted in the raging waters. Eventually, instead of reaching Portugal, the boat arrived in southern Italy at a place called Sicily.

Once on firm ground, Anthony was cared for by the brothers of his order who helped him back to health. Again and again he asked, "Lord God, I want to serve you totally. What do you want me to do?" He waited for God to show him.

At the end of May, there was a meeting of the Little Brothers near the town of Assisi. Anthony decided to attend. There he met Francis, the founder of his order.

After this meeting, the brothers returned to their communities. But Anthony didn't know where to go. He had not received an assignment like everyone else. Nobody knew him and nobody noticed him.

Finally, Anthony asked to be sent to a hermitage, a special place for prayer, in the mountains. Here, at last, he discovered what he had been looking for and what he needed: to be able to find himself and God in total quiet, in prayer, meditation and penance.

He lived a very simple life. He washed the dishes, cleaned the rooms, and took care of the yard. Who would think that this ordinary-looking brother, who did these little jobs, was an intelligent, educated priest?

Together with some of the other brothers, Anthony once traveled to the nearby town of Forli for an ordination. Many holy and well-known people gathered for this ceremony.

After the reading of the Gospel, someone suggested that one of the priests should preach a sermon. Imagine having to preach, without practicing, to such a big audience! No one wanted to try. The other priests were afraid to look foolish. One of them turned to Anthony. "Just tell them how God helps you," he said.

So Anthony stood up. He looked very calm and relaxed. Many people laughed. No one thought this young, unknown priest could possibly be a good speaker!

But what a surprise they had! Anthony spoke simply, from the bottom of his heart. The longer he spoke, the more the people were amazed. They saw the richness of his knowledge and his burning love for God.

Soon Anthony was sent to travel around the country and preach the Good News of the Gospel. In all kinds of weather, in all seasons, Anthony traveled across Italy. He bore the burning heat of the summers and the heavy rains and snow of the winters. Anthony taught the people all about God and strengthened them in their Christian faith. People crowded around him, forgetting even the time, their hunger and their tiredness but opening their hearts to God.

Anthony never worried about himself. His big concern was the good of others. He spent hours hearing their confessions and bringing them the peace and forgiveness of God. He had the gift of looking deep into people's hearts. He recognized their needs and their hidden sufferings. He comforted them and gave them hope.

Anthony's special friends were those who were poor or suffering. He used every ounce of his strength to improve their lives.

Anthony always stood up against cruelty and injustice.
He is called the "Father of the Poor," even today.

Of course, Anthony met problems, too. Certain persons didn't want to hear the Good News of Jesus. Their hearts were hard and closed. They even tried to poison Anthony. But God watched over him.

There is a story that one day, after some people wouldn't listen to him, Anthony went to the seashore to preach. The fish came in large numbers to hear him. They behaved very differently from the people! They seemed to understand what Anthony was saying. At the end of his sermon, the fish even nodded their heads to show that they agreed!

Another story tells about a meeting between Anthony and his opponents. One man said he was prepared to believe that the Holy Eucharist is really the Body and Blood of Jesus if Anthony could show him some proof. Everyone was sure that Anthony would lose the debate, unless a miracle happened.

A donkey which had not been fed for several days was led in. A large amount of food was placed by the donkey while Anthony walked towards the animal, carrying the Holy Eucharist.

Then an amazing thing happened—the starving donkey knelt down in front of the Holy Eucharist without paying any attention to the food!

From Northern Italy, Anthony's journeys took him to France. There he was asked to spend some time preaching and teaching at the universities of Montpellier and Toulouse. He spoke out against the wrong ideas about God which were being spread in the south of France.

After Francis died, Anthony had to return to Italy. He had been given an important job in the Franciscan Order. He settled in the city of Padua. Until the end of his life, Anthony preached there. Even today, just hearing the name of this city makes us think of him.

Anthony was still a young man, but he was totally exhausted from his long journeys and his preaching. He really needed rest and some time alone.

Summer was near, with its sweltering heat, and Anthony had to leave Padua. Count Tiso, a good friend of his, gave him a hermitage in the country where he settled with some of his Franciscan brothers.

Now Anthony could finally have some silence and time alone for prayer and meditation. Count Tiso built him a tree house. Anthony enjoyed staying there to pray and write about God.

One day Count Tiso watched as Anthony knelt before a statue of the Infant Jesus, gently kissed the divine Child and begged to be taken to paradise soon. Then Anthony told Count Tiso a secret: the Infant Jesus had appeared to him several times while he was meditating on Jesus' humanity and childhood.

After a while, Anthony became very ill. He asked to be taken back to the convent in Padua, where he wished to die. He was put on a cart. In the stifling heat, his brothers took him back along a path which is known today as "the Saint's road."

Anthony was so sick that they couldn't make it to Padua and had to stop at a nearby monastery. In the presence of his brothers, he received the sacraments. After this his eyes lit up and he exclaimed, "I see my Lord!"

Anthony died on June 13, 1231, at the age of 36.

His body was taken back to Padua, where a large crowd was waiting for him. His death had been announced to them immediately in a mysterious way. The children of the city had started running through the streets, calling out, "The Holy One has died! Our saint has died!"

Exactly one year after Anthony's death, Pope Gregory IX officially declared him a saint. We celebrate the feast of Saint Anthony every year on June 13.

This picture shows the huge church which was built in honor of Anthony in the city of Padua. But devotion to Saint Anthony quickly spread from Padua, so that soon he became the "Saint of the whole world."

Saint Anthony is still very important today. He lives with God and prays for each of us.

Amazing numbers of people from all over the world still visit Padua every year. They come to honor Anthony who always sang the praises of God and the Virgin Mary, whom he called his "Mother in Heaven."

They come to honor Anthony who loved and protected the poor, as his Franciscan brothers continue to do today.

If we ask him to, Saint Anthony will be very happy to help us love and live as he did!

Some interesting facts about Saint Anthony...

Even after going to heaven, Anthony of Padua still helps people here on earth. He is often called upon when something lost or misplaced needs to be found in a hurry. Maybe you have heard someone groan, "Where did I leave my glasses?" Or "I can't find my keys! What am I going to do? Saint Anthony, please help me!" Would you like to know why we ask for Saint Anthony's help when we try to find something we've lost? It's because one day, while Anthony was living in France, a novice ran away from the monastery and took with him a book that belonged to Anthony. The book was an explanation of the psalms, which he himself had written. Anthony prayed to get his book back and soon it was returned!

The "Alms of Anthony," or "St. Anthony's Bread"

In memory of Anthony's good deeds and his care for the poor, generous people often give gifts to those who need them most. This is called the "Alms of Anthony" or "St. Anthony's Bread." This money is always used for the poor. A priest may use it to help an unemployed father buy food for his family and pay their rent. Or a poor mother might be able to buy medicine and warm clothes for her child with it. There are many other good uses for these generous gifts.

Anthony and the Gospel

When you read the Gospel, you find that Jesus said to his disciples, "I was hungry and you fed me." And then Jesus explained, "Whatever you did for one of my brothers, you did for me." You can imagine how Anthony enjoyed helping the hungry, the poor and the sick, just as if he were serving Jesus himself.

The statue of Saint Anthony

Look closely at the statue of Saint Anthony. He is often shown holding the Infant Jesus in his arms. This reminds us of the vision he had near the end of his life.

Saint Anthony, Patron Saint of the Church of Portugal

Saint Anthony, the little Portuguese boy Fernando, has become the Patron Saint of the Church in Portugal. There are also many churches around the world dedicated to him.

Doctor of the Church

Anthony is not only a "Saint." Pope Pius XII also gave him the title "Doctor of the Church." ("Doctor" here means "Teacher.") He is called this because of how well he spread the Good News of Jesus' Gospel.

A few words to help you better understand St. Anthony's life . . .

Abbot:
The name given to the monk who governs a monastery.

Canonize:
The act by which the Pope, in the name of the Catholic Church, declares that a person is a saint, after serious research into that person's life and holiness.

Hermitage:
A house far from other homes, set aside for prayer.

Holy Eucharist:
The real Body and Blood of the risen Jesus present under the appearances of bread and wine at Mass. The Holy Eucharist is also kept, in the form of the consecrated hosts, in the tabernacle.

Martyr:
A person who is killed because of his or her faith.

Monastery:
The name given to the house where monks live.

Novice:
A person learning to live in a religious order.

Saint Francis of Assisi:
A holy man who began the "Little Brothers," now called the Franciscan Order. He was canonized a saint in the year 1228.

Prayer

Saint Anthony,
you loved God very much.
Please, help me to love God
more and more
and to share his love
with everyone I meet.
You always tried to obey God.
Help me to do whatever
God asks of me.
Lead me along the paths of the Gospel,
in the footsteps of Jesus.
Teach me to be good and kind to others,
to help them and never to ignore
a poor or sad person.
Saint Anthony,
you who are so close to God,
pray for me
and for all the people of the world.

Amen.

BOOKS & MEDIA

The Daughters of St. Paul operate book and media centers at the following addresses. Visit, call or write the one nearest you today, or find us on the World Wide Web, www.pauline.org

CALIFORNIA
3908 Sepulveda Blvd., Culver City, CA 90230; 310-397-8676
5945 Balboa Ave., San Diego, CA 92111; 619-565-9181
46 Geary Street, San Francisco, CA 94108; 415-781-5180

FLORIDA
145 S.W. 107th Ave., Miami, FL 33174; 305-559-6715

HAWAII
1143 Bishop Street, Honolulu, HI 96813; 808-521-2731

ILLINOIS
172 North Michigan Ave., Chicago, IL 60601; 312-346-4228

LOUISIANA
4403 Veterans Memorial Blvd., Metairie, LA 70006; 504-887-7631

MASSACHUSETTS
50 St. Paul's Ave., Jamaica Plain, Boston, MA 02130; 617-522-8911
Rte. 1, 885 Providence Hwy., Dedham, MA 02026; 781-326-5385

MISSOURI
9804 Watson Rd., St. Louis, MO 63126; 314-965-3512

NEW JERSEY
561 U.S. Route 1, Wick Plaza, Edison, NJ 08817; 732-572-1200

NEW YORK
150 East 52nd Street, New York, NY 10022; 212-754-1110
78 Fort Place, Staten Island, NY 10301; 718-447-5071

OHIO
2105 Ontario Street, Cleveland, OH 44115; 440-621-9427

PENNSYLVANIA
9171-A Roosevelt Blvd., Philadelphia, PA 19114; 215-676-9494

SOUTH CAROLINA
243 King Street, Charleston, SC 29401; 843-577-0175

TENNESSEE
4811 Poplar Ave., Memphis, TN 38117; 901-761-2987

TEXAS
114 Main Plaza, San Antonio, TX 78205; 210-224-8101

VIRGINIA
1025 King Street, Alexandria, VA 22314; 703-549-3806

CANADA
3022 Dufferin Street, Toronto, Ontario, Canada M6B 3T5; 416-781-9131
1155 Yonge Street, Toronto, Ontario, Canada M4T 1W2; 416-934-3440